For John Tomanio, my prime friend.—E.M.

To Andreas from H.D.

Copyright © 1992 Rabbit Ears Productions. Inc., Rowayton, Connecticut.
Rabbit Ears Books is an imprint of Rabbit Ears Productions.
Published by Picture Book Studio Ltd., Saxonville, Massachusetts.
Distributed in the United States by Simon & Schuster.
Distributed in Canada by Vanwell Publishing, St. Catharines, Ontario.
All rights reserved.
Printed in Hong Kong.
10 9 8 7 6 5 4 3 2 1

Library of Congress Cataloging in Publication Data
Metaxas, Eric
The fool and the flying ship/written by Eric Metaxas; illustrated by Henrik Drescher.
p. cm.
Summary; When the Tsar proclaims that he will marry his daughter to the man who brings him a flying ship, a goofy coutry bumpkin
sets out to try his luck and meets some unusual companions on the way. Includes an audio cassette with narration and music.
ISBN 0-88708-228-9.—ISBN 0-88708-229-7 (book and cassette package).
[1. Fairy tales. 2. Folklore—Soviet Union.] I. Drescher, Henrik, ill. II. Title.
PZ8.M55Fo 1992
398.21′0947—dc20
[E]   91-40669
CIP
AC

The Fool & the Flying Ship

Written by Eric Metaxas   Illustrated by Henrik Drescher

Rabbit Ears Books

nce, a while ago, there was an old peasant and his wife and their three sons. Two of the boys were quite clever, but the third son, alas, was not.

Now it came to pass in those days that the Tsar of all Russia issued a proclamation to every cottage in the land that whosoever could build a flying ship, one that could sail throughout the blue sky, this way and that, hither and yon, yon and hither, would win the hand of his lovely daughter, the princess. ✦ The two clever brothers were naturally eager to try their luck and so they each resolved to set off. ✦ Their father gladly provided them finer clothes than he had ever worn himself and gave his blessing for their journey. Their mother made up hampers of food—soft white rolls, cooked meats, bottles of corn brandy, and a little potato latke—maybe for later. ✦ The Fool saw all this and he said he would go along too, for he wished to receive such fine things and his father's blessings, but his cruel brothers only knocked his cap off and teased him.

✤ "Imagine the Tsar's daughter marrying that circus ape!" they said as they were leaving. ✤ Even after they had walked away a good ways down the road, the poor Fool could hear them guffawing loudly. Still, for all their cleverness, they were never heard from again.

Some time passed, not much, and not a little, and the Fool decided his time to leave had come. But when he told his mother she only scoffed. ✣ "Ha!" she said. "With your fine luck it's only a matter of hours before you're eaten by a pack of wolves!" ✣ But his father was of a different mind. "If he is eaten, then he is eaten. It's high time we allowed the boy to learn by his own mistakes."

✣ "Your father may have a kind heart toward you," his mother said, being the good woman that she was, "but as for me, if you are eaten by wild beasts, don't even think about coming home!" ✣ And with that she gave him some old rusks she'd thrown into a sack and he left. ✣ The Fool had not gone far into the woods when he met an ancient wisp of a man leaning on a rude crutch. ✣ The man had a wild icicle of a beard and a pair of lively white eyebrows that leapt like snowhares when he spoke. ✣ "Where goest thou, young fellow?" he asked. ✣ "Truth be told, I'm going to marry the Tsar's daughter— but first I must build a flying ship." ✣ "How will you do that?" the old man asked. ✣ But the Fool had not yet thought that far. ✣ "Well then," said the old man. "Let's rest a bit and have a bite to eat." ✣ "I am ashamed to offer you what I have here," said the Fool. "It's good enough for me, but certainly not the sort of meal to which one asks guests— although if you are hungry I'll be more than happy to share what I have."

And so he began to unpack his meager fare, but as he did so, his eyes blossomed wide with surprise. There was wine and corn brandy and soft, white rolls, and all manner of cooked meats and sausages and delicate cheeses–the kind of cheeses that just take you by the nose and lead you around the house! There was even a tin of caviar made from a pair of fish that swam only in champagne! And all the plates were made of the finest silver and engraved with scenes of soldiers in battle so lifelike that if one looked closely one could imagine one

heard the sound of gunfire! ✤ The two of them dined on this great repast until they could eat no more, and before long, the Fool fell sound asleep against a large tree. ✤ When he awoke he discovered that he was not leaning against a tree, no, but against the smooth hull of a great ship, and the old man was nowhere to be seen. ✤ "My, my...I can hardly remember being so industrious," thought the Fool, "but look what I've done!" ✤ And he danced happily around the ship admiring his handiwork. He quickly jumped aboard and seized the tiller. Instantly the ship leapt into the air and shot away over the treetops. ✤ Before long he spotted a very thin fellow carrying a roasted pig.

✤ "Good day to you, Uncle Skinny," said the Fool. "Where
are you going?" ✤ "Why, to buy some dinner." ✤ "But
there's a banquet under your nose!" the Fool called out.
✤ "Really?" the man said. "Where? Oh, why this, this is
just a scrap—hardly a mouthful." ✤ "I'm on my way to
marry the Tsar's daughter. There's sure to be a good deal
to eat there! Come aboard!" ✤ So the Big Eater climbed
aboard and they sped off.

They flew on and on until looking down at the earth below the Fool saw a man with ears the size of soup plates lying with one of his ears pressed to the ground. ✛ "Good day to you!" the Fool shouted to him. "What are you doing down there?" ✛ "Not so loud! I am listening to an ant coughing in Ethiopia. And it's quite a terrible cough he has!" ✛ "Why, you have rather good hearing to hear insects coughing all the way in Ethiopia!" ✛ "Yes," said the man. "And it would be a real cinch—if only his wife weren't such a terrific snorer. What a racket! I wonder if he's not dead with such an infernal hubbub!" ✛ "Well, come aboard," said the Fool. "We're going to the wedding of the Tsar's daughter, and you're sure to get an earful there!" ✛ And so the man came aboard and they sped off over the hills. ✛ Before long they spotted a man hopping along on one foot, with the other tied behind his head. ✛ "Ahoy there, Lord Pegleg!" cried the Fool. "Why are you hopping along on one foot?" ✛ "And what would you have me do on one foot?" the man asked. "Pirouette? Besides, if I were to untie my other foot I would move too fast for anyone to see me. Why, I would trip over the equator in one stride." ✛ "That's pretty quick," the Fool said. ✛ "If you think that's quick," the man replied, " you should have seen me before the old arthritis set in." ✛ "Come aboard," said the Fool. "We're headed for the wedding of the Tsar's daughter—he's sure to require a speedy messenger!" ✛ And off they went.

hey flew on and on until down by the roadside they saw a man aiming a gun whose barrel was the length of two plough horses and a clever she-goat. ✤ "Ahoy there, William Tellsky!" the Fool shouted. "Can you tell us what you're aiming at?" ✤ "Well, you see," the man said, rubbing his jaw, "there's an ant in Ethiopia with a terrible cough. I should like to put him out of his misery." ✤ "But it's his wife's loud snoring that keeps him ill!" the Fool replied. ✤ "Yes, of course," the man replied. "She's the one I'm aiming for!" ✤ "Take your place among us," said the Fool. "The Tsar is sure to require such a skilled marksman!" ✤ So the Sharp-shooter hopped aboard and they sped away. ✤ As they were traveling they saw a shrunken weakling of a man stooped beneath a head of hair so great that he groaned with the effort of carrying it. ✤ "Ahoy there, Cousin Hunchback!" the Fool shouted. "What sort of burden have you got there?" ✤ "It's no burden at all," he replied wearily. "It's only my strength I'm carrying, and there's quite a lot of it as you can see!"

✤ "Well, there's going to be a wedding of the Tsar's daughter," said the Fool. "And they're sure to need a strong man there. In any case, they're sure to have a pair of shears for a decent haircut! Climb aboard, Samson!"

✤ But the weakling couldn't manage it himself, so the Fool and the Sharp-shooter got down and lent him a hand, pulled him up onto the ship, and they sailed across the countryside.

hey didn't meet anyone else on their journey and after some time had passed, not much and not a little, they came to the palace of the Tsar himself. The Tsar was at that moment eating his dinner, which, tightwad that he was, consisted of no more than a tiny bowl of borscht without any sour cream. ✦ He and his daughter, the princess, looked out the window to see where the noise was coming from and saw the strange ship descending with its giddy crew making crude gestures and waving boisterously at them. ✦ One of the Tsar's servants—a miniature genius interested in marrying the Tsar's daughter himself—was watering his mechanical bear at the fountain when the ship landed. ✦ Now the Tsar thought that there was no one in the world worthy of his daughter's hand in marriage— although he secretly hoped that the Prince of the Moon would come in a flying ship. But if no one came after a certain time, well, he had promised the small servant his daughter's hand.

On seeing the flying ship, the servant immediately perceived that the ship's crew were just a rough group of simple peasants, not the Prince of the Moon, and he quickly went running into the Tsar's dining room, huffing and puffing. ✤ "Has the Prince of the Moon come for the hand of my lovely daughter?" the Tsar asked the servant, beaming with pride. ✤ "Far from it, your majesty," replied the winded egghead. "It's just a loud group of simple moujiks—moujiks every one of them!" ✤ "Moujiks. Right. What's a moujik?" the Tsar asked. ✤ "Peasants, your majesty." ✤ "Pheasants?" ✤ "No! Peasants, just a group of low-lifes from the countryside. And the leader of this riff-raff claims he's fulfilled the requirements of your proclamation with that ship of his. And he's asked for the hand of your daughter, the princess!" ✤ "Uh-oh," said the Tsar, visibly shaken. "Er, could I see that proclamation again?" ✤ "Yes, your majesty," said the smarty-pants, immediately producing the parchment. "There it is in black and white." ✤ "Whoops. Well, I suppose we're in a jam all right..."

So the servant, the Tsar and the princess sat for a while in complete silence, considering their dilemma. ✥ "I have it, your majesty!" the servant cried, "perhaps you can set this rogue and his gang three impossible tasks—ones they can never fulfill!" ✥ "Now we're getting somewhere," said the Tsar. "Like what?" ✥ "You could ask them to eat a thousand loaves of bread!" the servant replied. ✥ This nearly tore the Tsar in two. He wanted desperately to rid himself of this unwanted suitor, but, as a tightwad, the idea of parting

with a thousand loaves of bread was more than he could bear! But in the end, to get rid of the Fool, he agreed. ✥ And so the servant went to the Fool, who was turning somersaults and cracking jokes with his party, and brought him into the palace. ✥ "Aha!" said the Fool loudly on seeing the princess. "My bride-to-be! What a vision you are! And my soon-to-be father-in-law! May I call you Pop?" ✥ "Pop?!" said the Tsar, reddening. ✥ "Ahem, it is his majesty's desire that all suitors first fulfill three small tasks before any wedding plans be discussed," the servant said.

 e then produced a huge volume nearly as large as he was and pretended to consult it carefully. ✤ "Ah, yes. To begin with, you and your hick crew must first eat not less than one thousand loaves of bread!" ✤ "I'm afraid none of my men is very hungry right now," the Fool said, "but perhaps I can persuade one of them to try with me." ✤ So he summoned the Eater from the ship, and no sooner than the loaves were set before them they were gone. ✤ "I think I have some loaves coming to me yet," the Eater said anxiously. "I'm afraid it only tasted like nine hundred, really—I'm quite sure of it."

ow the Tsar was more upset than ever, as you can imagine, and his daughter, the princess, was biting her lip. But the servant was as sly as a fox, and he again thought quickly. ✤ "Excellent, excellent. And now," he said as he pretended again to read from the book, "let me see... Ah, yes. You must journey down to Africa and fetch a piece of the equator! Then the Tsar's daughter will be yours!" ✤ And he and the Tsar chuckled at the Fool, who seemed to be thinking the matter over. ✤ "A piece of the equator, eh?" the Fool said. "Any particular size piece?" ✤ The Tsar and the servant looked at each other uncomfortably. ✤ "Size!?" stammered the servant. "Er, not really, but you must bring it before sundown— and not a minute later!" ✤ "Well, you probably know what it's like to run about on a full stomach," the Fool replied calmly. "So if you have no objection I will ask one of my courtiers to make the journey." ✤ And so he arose from the table, went into the courtyard and described the situation. ✤ "This is my affair," said the Runner, who stood up, quickly untied the leg from behind his head and began to wiggle it to get the stiffness out.

The very instant in which he touched it to the ground he was out of sight—and just as he predicted, he tripped over the equator in his first stride and fell headlong into deepest Africa.

✥ When he got up, he immediately retied his leg and began to hop along the equator's length, for he hoped to scout out a nice, handsome piece. Now, as everyone knows who's been there, the equator is a bright blue color, with worm-like imperfections here and there, because it's been drawn so many times on a map.

❖ When he came upon a part of it that was free of imperfections and was so brilliantly blue that it made the sky look as red as a rose in comparison, he bit off a nice piece the size of a young fig, put it in his pocket, and sat down against a tree to take a nap.

During the time that the Runner was gone, the Fool was conversing with the Tsar and princess. After some time though, he wondered where his friend was, and so he went out to the ship. ✧ "Oho!" said the Hearer, with his ear to the ground. "Our swift pal has fallen asleep under a tree! I can hear him snoring—and there's a flea asleep in the hair on the very top of his head, just ten rows back from the widow's peak—wait, no sorry, twelve—and the flea's snoring too!" ✧ "I see him!" said the Sharp-shooter. "I see him!" ✧ "Who, Lord Pegleg?" asked the Fool. ✧ "No, the flea. Ah, now I see Pegleg, just below the flea. Leave it to me!" ✧ The Sharp-shooter quickly picked up his rifle, aimed carefully and— allowing for wind, curvature and spin of the earth, continental drift and the expansion of the universe, and the chance that he might sneeze—squeezed the trigger. The bullet hit the flea squarely amidships—which is to say it struck the third button on his brocaded flea's vest, a dead bull's-eye, and ricocheted loudly off the embossed buckle on his high-heeled shoe. Not a bad shot. ✧ The sound was so loud that it immediately woke the Runner, who, seeing that the sun was about to set, quickly put both feet on the ground, and faster than sixty-three speeding bullets, arrived at the Tsar's palace with the equator safely in his pocket. ✧ He gave it to the Fool, who immediately brought it in to the Tsar and his daughter.

ow the Tsar began growing quite pale, and his daughter was crossing and uncrossing her eyes unattractively—but again the servant thought quickly. ✤ "This is all well and good," he said, winking at the Tsar. "But there is yet one more task listed which you must fulfill." ✤ And again he pretended to read from the large book. ✤ "Ah, yes. You must find a bird that cannot fly, yet loves to swim, and has nary a single feather on it's body—and you must fetch it here by sun-up tomorrow! Good night!" ✤ So the Fool returned to the ship and related the situation. Now, naturally, the Eater was aware of all the birds in the world that could be eaten, and he said that he had heard of such birds as the servant described—but he said that they lived at the very bottom of the world, far beyond the equator, where it was very cold. ✤ So the Sharp-shooter immediately looked in that direction and with a little squinting said: ✤ "Aha! I see some birds who cannot fly and have no feathers! But when they dive into the water, they stay underneath, and I cannot see them swimming!" ✤ So the Hearer put his ear to the ground and with a little straining said: ✤ "I can hear those birds with no feathers who cannot fly, and I hear their wings flapping underwater as they swim!" ✤ That settled it. Of course the Runner was again eager to make the journey and fetch the bird, and he was already beginning to untie his leg—but the Sharp-shooter objected strongly. ✤ "No, no, no!" he said to them. "You see, I have run out of bullets! If the Runner should fall asleep again we'll be quite powerless to rouse him! He simply cannot go!" ✤ So they sat there silently, thinking.

ut just one-tenth of a second before they were about to give up, the hairy weakling clambered up out of the ship's hold, and blinked at the twilight, for he had been sleeping soundly below decks since their arrival.   ✤ "I perceive it's high time I puffed up," he announced to them weakly. "Yes, yes, time to puff up indeed."   ✤ And immediately he began to inhale quite vigorously—so vigorously, in fact, that anything that was not tied down was soon sucked into his lungs. And as he did this, a very strange thing took place.   ✤ His puny body began to inflate, while at the same time his oppressive mane began to retreat back into his head! And by the time he was through he was as big and strong as he had been small and weak and his pate was as shiny as a shaved melon!   ✤ "I thought you'd look better with a haircut!" said the Fool, turning a handspring.   ✤ The Puffer then opined that if they were unprepared to travel to the South Pole, they would have to bring the South Pole to them.

And so, grabbing ahold of a piece of turf, he began quickly hauling the countryside toward himself like sailcloth! ✤ The Fool and his crew watched in absolute amazement as houses and whole villages appeared on the horizon like ships, came toward them, and then disappeared into the pile behind the Puffer! ✤ As daylight left them, entire countries passed before their eyes, their inhabitants going about their lives as though everything were completely normal—whole families passing by them. On and on it went! Faster and faster the Puffer pulled, never stopping! He pulled and pulled, all through the night, on and on and on! ✤ Finally, just as he was running out of strength and the first rays of the sun were beginning to redden the horizon, the South Pole skidded to a halt, right in the center of the Tsar's courtyard! And his job was done. ✤ Now, when the Tsar woke up, he immediately looked out his window. There in the courtyard below he beheld hundreds and hundreds of penguins waddling about and swimming in the

courtyard fountain, while behind the Puffer lay the entire earth in a single wrinkled pile! ✤ And who should be standing on his head atop the South Pole in the center of the courtyard? Who indeed, but the Fool himself! ✤ Of course the Tsar shook with fear at all that he saw, for what could he do? Without a moment's hesitation he threw open his bedroom window and shouted down to the Fool: ✤ "Congratulations, my dear son-in-law, she's all yours!"

And so the Fool and the princess were married that very morning, and the Tsar gave the Fool half of his kingdom, and fired his pint-sized servant, while the companions in the flying ship took up the best quarters in the palace. They were forever by his side, cracking jokes and singing songs, and they and the Fool were very happy. ✤ Oh, and as for the princess—well, maybe she got used to it.